A Wave in Her Pocket

STORIES FROM TRINIDAD

A Wave in Her Pocket

STORIES FROM TRINIDAD

by Lynn Joseph
Illustrated by Brian Pinkney

CLARION BOOKS

New York

The author acknowledges Gerard Besson's *Folklore and Legends of Trinidad and Tobago* (Port-of-Spain, Trinidad: Paria Publishing Company, Ltd., 1989) for background information on Trinidad's folklore.

Clarion Books
a Houghton Mifflin Company imprint
215 Park Avenue South, New York, NY 10003
Text copyright © 1991 by Lynn Joseph
Illustrations copyright © 1991 by Brian Pinkney

For information about this and other Houghton Mifflin trade
and reference books and multimedia products, visit The Bookstore at
Houghton Mifflin on the World Wide Web at (http://www.hmco.com/trade/).

Printed in the USA

Library of Congress Cataloging-in-Publication Data
Joseph, Lynn.
A wave in her pocket: stories from Trinidad / by Lynn Joseph ;
illustrated by Brian Pinkney.
p.   cm.
Summary: On the island of Trinidad, Tantie tells the children six
stories, some originating in the countries of West Africa, some in
Trinidad, and some in her own imagination.
ISBN 0-395-54432-7   PA ISBN 0-395-81309-3
1. Tales—Trinidad   [1. Folklore—Trinidad.]   I. Pinkney,
Brian, ill.   II. Title.
PZ8. 1.J76Wav   1991
398.2—dc20
[E]   90-39359
CIP
AC

HOR 10 9 8 7 6 5

For my mother, Janette,
with love

Contents

Note

Almost all families in Trinidad have a tantie. A tantie is usually a grandaunt who helps to take care of all the grandnephews and grandnieces. She often gives advice to mothers on raising children even if she herself has no children. On family outings she entertains the children by gathering them all together and telling them stories. Sometimes she tells stories to teach them a lesson. Sometimes she tells stories to scare them or make them laugh. But the main thing about a tantie's stories is that she always has one ready, because any time is story time.

Many of the stories that tanties tell originate in the countries of West Africa. Others begin right in Trinidad. And some tanties make up stories that no one else has ever told before.

Here are some of my tantie's best stories, remembered forever.

A Wave in Her Pocket

STORIES FROM TRINIDAD

A Soucouyant Dies

EVERY YEAR MY DADDY'S FAMILY has a big beach picnic at Mayaro Bay. Daddy, Mama, and I arrive early in the morning. Daddy's eight brothers and sisters are already there. My five uncles set up the coal pots and gather sticks for the fire. My aunts unpack the food. I smell Auntie Hazel's tangy coconut bread all the way from the road.

Some of my cousins climb the coconut tree that leans over the water. Some pound the cricket wickets into the sand. My favorite cousins, Avril, Cedric, Susan, and Gerard, usually stand near Tantie. Tantie is the only person who just sits down.

When I run up Tantie will say, "Morning, Amber."

I will give a little curtsey. On my island we curtsey or bow when we say hello to important people. And Tantie is *very* important. She's the one who tells the stories!

At last year's picnic though, Tantie did more than just tell a story. She cause a big bacchanal and scare everybody.

It started when Tantie stood at the edge of the sea and shouted, "Which one of you is a soucouyant?"

None of us knew what Tantie was talking 'bout, but a soucouyant is nothing to make joke with! It's a ball of fire that flies through the air and will suck the blood clean out of you.

My cousin Avril, who is the bravest one in our little group, asked Tantie, "Whatcha talkin' 'bout so? Who is a soucouyant?"

Tantie didn't pay him no mind. She just looked at the sea and laughed.

At lunchtime, when the sand was so hot it burn up our feet, we all sat under the coconut trees. Tantie tied a big red kerchief around her waist. We thought it was a napkin.

But then she tied tiny bells onto the ends of the kerchief. "They'll ring when de soucouyant comes near," she said.

Cedric, who is nine years old, like me, went and sat by Tantie to listen for the bells. But Tantie got up and stamped her foot at him. "Which one of you is de soucouyant?" she shouted.

"Tantie, you know we are not soucouyants," he said. "Not us!"

Tantie's bells rang a tiny bit and she looked at the sea and laughed.

It was a scary laugh and I couldn't stop thinking about it all afternoon as I played cricket and dug for chip-chips in the wet sand. Daddy had promised to made his famous chip-chip soup with the meat from the tiny shells. But I couldn't think much about Daddy's soup. I could hear Tantie's voice in the back of my mind asking, "Which one of you is de soucouyant?"

I looked over at Mama resting by the sea, at Auntie Hazel reading a book, and at Uncle Rupert cutting open coconuts. I looked at baby James sleeping on his soft bed of leaves. None of them looked like a soucouyant to me. What in the world was Tantie talking about?

Then the sun went down. Hundreds of stars shone through the coconut leaves. A little moon slid up into the sky.

Daddy, Mama, and my aunts and uncles packed up the coal pots. "We coming back later," they said. And off they went for their walk, leaving Tantie with us.

Tantie sat down on the sand. Me and my cousins sat around her.

"Tantie, you going to tell us about de soucouyant?" Avril asked.

Tantie nodded her head and her bells rang softly. The coconut trees bent down their heads and made huge, scary faces on the sand.

Then Tantie began: "Once, a long time ago, an old woman from this very family of ours lived at de end of a village road. She never had any visitors and she didn't want any either. All day long this old woman slept. But when de sun went down into de sea and de birds in de old trees over her house turned into bats, de old woman awoke."

Tantie's bells started ringing, but she went on with her story. "De woman woke up and started peeling off her skin, one piece at a time. Then she bundled up her skin and put it all in a cold stone jug. Now she was a ball of fire—a soucouyant. She hid de jug where no one could find it. Slowly, so that she wouldn't touch anything in de house and catch it on fire, de soucouyant rose up through de roof.

"'Shreeeeeee,' she cried as de village dogs began howling. And off she flew.

"Villagers far and wide were terrified of de soucouyant. No one was safe walking home from market at night. Anyone who had far to walk had to close up his stall early. De villagers knew that de soucouyant waited for anyone foolish enough to walk alone at night. If she found anyone, she'd fly down and cover him up with fire, then suck de blood clean out of him."

Tantie's bells were ringing a little louder now, but she didn't seem to notice. She continued: "One day, a young boy, new to de village, heard about de soucouyant. He set out for de old woman's house at de edge of de village road. He had a plan. He waited in de bushes till de sun went down and de birds had changed into bats. Then he watched carefully as de soucouyant hid her stone jug of skin on a high shelf.

"As soon as de soucouyant rose up through de roof, de boy ran to her hiding place and took down de jug of skin. In his pocket was a bag filled with de coarse salt that villagers used to cure goat meat and ham. He sprinkled it all over de skin. Then he ran home before de soucouyant could see him from de night sky.

"As night faded, de soucouyant flew swiftly through the forest toward her home. She took down de jug and tried to put on her skin. But something was wrong! It burned like fire. It shrank and slid away. And de soucouyant wailed, 'Skin kin kin, you na no me? You na no me?' She had to get back into her skin before de sun rose.

"She pleaded with de dreadful skin that kept sliding off of her. 'You na no me, old skin?'

"Then she realized what must have been done. And as de sun rose slowly over de trees, de soucouyant's ball of flame died down to nothing. De day had dawned before she could return to her skin.

"That night, de villagers threw a big party and everyone rejoiced."

As Tantie finished telling her story, her bells rang even louder than before.

"But how can de bells ring?" cried my cousin Susan, who is a scaredy-cat. "De soucouyant is gone."

In the moonlight Tantie's face looked frightened. "Yes," she whispered. "*That* soucouyant is gone. But what those villagers didn't know is that every fifty years a new soucouyant rises up in this family of ours. Today is fifty years since de old woman sang her song, 'Skin kin kin, you na no me?'"

Tantie's bells rang louder and louder and we held onto each other's hands tightly.

Suddenly, a small burst of flame flew up and over the coconut trees. There was a loud scream. I ran behind a rock. I could hear Avril and Gerard yelling and Tantie's bells ringing and someone or something crashing through the trees close to where I was hiding. "De soucouyant is coming," I said to myself.

Then above all the shouting and carrying on, I heard Mama's voice. And Daddy's and Uncle Rupert's and Auntie Hazel's and the rest of them. I peeked out from behind my rock and saw them shining torchlights at the trees. "Come on, children," they said. "Tantie was just telling one of her little stories. No big thing to be scared of."

One by one we came out from our hiding places. Auntie Hazel was asking, "Why you must scare de children so, Tantie?"

Tantie never answered. I think that was because of what she and me and my cousins knew. Even though our mothers and fathers took us home and tucked us safely into our beds, me and my cousins never forgot that ball of flame that flew up past the coconut trees when Tantie's bells were ringing loud loud. We never figured out which one of us was the soucouyant either.

Ligahoo

EVERY YEAR STARTING IN MAY, the rainy season comes and sits like a heavy bushel basket on my head. With the rain comes Auntie Hazel to keep Mama company. Auntie Hazel is Cedric's and Susan's mother. The best part about her coming over is that Cedric and Susan come too. Then Avril, who lives right down the street from me, joins us. We could have plenty of fun then, except that now we have two grown-ups telling us no instead of only one.

No, we can't go to Maracas Bay where the waves are big. No, we can't play cricket in the Savannah. And no, we can't go down to Four Roads River and watch the tadpoles turn into baby frogs.

"With all this rain, that river could overflow anytime," says Auntie Hazel, with her hands on her big hips.

"No playing by de river," says Mama, shaking a long finger at us.

But like cousin Avril used to say, "What else is there to do during de rainy season 'cept watch de river water rise high high and see if de place flood?"

So that's just what we'd do. After the long morning rain, we'd wait until Mama and Auntie Hazel fell asleep on the back porch. Then we'd tiptoe out the front door and run down to the river.

The riverbanks are yellow and wide and slant down to the river-bed. In the dry season, snails and frogs crawl and hop about. And the river is small enough for us to jump across. But in the rainy season, the river grows fat and full. Sometimes the water climbs all the way up the slanted yellow bank and out into the streets.

Most times during the rainy season we'd just stand on the river-bank and watch the thick, red-brown water swoosh on by, carrying tree branches and old tires.

One day though, Tantie changed all that. She was visiting, and we thought she was asleep like Mama and Auntie Hazel on the back porch.

The afternoon was smelling clean and fresh from the rain and the sun was shining strong strong on our backs. Avril, Cedric, Susan, and I stood on the riverbank squishing the muddy grass into little points with our toes. Two big rainbows filled up the sky with Carnival colors. Everything was quiet except for the river, which was groaning like an old cow horn.

Then all of a sudden we heard a voice behind us. "All yuh must be waiting to see Ligahoo?"

We spin around so fast we almost tumbled down into the river.

Avril was the first one to speak. "Tantie," he said, "what you doing here? We thought you sleeping like everyone else."

It was the wrong thing to say. Tantie face set up and she say, "I look like an old fool to you, chile? I know all yuh children were going to come check on de river. But I didn't know you'd be wait-ing for Ligahoo."

"Tantie, who's Ligahoo?" I asked, feeling a tiny bit scared in case Ligahoo was someone like the soucouyant.

"We not waiting for anybody," said Cedric, who is always truthful.

"Chile, shhh," Tantie said and put a finger to her lips. "Ligahoo not a *anybody*. If he hear you talking so, I don't know what could happen. Last time Ligahoo get vex he cause a flood worse than de madness on de first day of Carnival."

Tantie wrung her hands and then she picked up the hem of her dress and bent down to wipe her face. "I can feel Ligahoo right here," she said.

"Where?" I asked.

"Down there," Tantie said, pointing to the brown rushing water.

"Tantie, ain't nobody down there," said Cedric, peering over the edge.

Tantie closed her eyes and shook her head. "I see all yuh never meet up with Ligahoo before. Or maybe all yuh did and didn't know him."

"What he look like?" I asked.

Tantie smiled a mysterious smile. "Ligahoo," she said, "can look like anything he wants."

Then she began walking away from the riverbank. We followed behind her because Tantie had that look on her face that means a story coming.

"Near here," she started, "there lives a man who knows more than anyone else. He knows how to cure bellyaches. He knows how to put goat mouth on people just by saying their name, so then something bad happens to them. He even know how to tell de river what to do. That man is de one we call Ligahoo."

"How does he tell de river what to do?" whispered Susan.

Tantie laughed. Then her face got serious. "We must be very respectful," she said. "Ligahoo has power over many things. When

Ligahoo was a young man just learning about his powers, this island had so much confusion. Nobody knew what Ligahoo would do next. One night all streetlights went out and de whole place in darkness till morning. Another time, de island shook like crazy and trees and lampposts fell down. And another time, Ligahoo get vex 'cause we didn't want to make him King of the Carnival, so he make a storm rage over de place for three days with rain and thunder and lightning. Nobody dare go out in de street to jump up, so Carnival cancel that year. That was when we realize that Ligahoo mean business. After that ain't nobody so much as stick out a big toe against him.

"Ligahoo is de one that set up this six-months rain, six-months dry plan. And is he self say that we cahn come down to de river during rainy season."

Tantie smiled then like the story finish, but I knew my cousins were wondering the same thing I was. So I asked Tantie, "Why Ligahoo don't want nobody to see de river?"

"Because," she answered, "de river is Ligahoo's home in de rainy season. De scary thing about Ligahoo is that he can change his shape to be any animal he wants. His favorite is de fish, so every year he spends six months being a fish in de river. And he don't like people to come down to his home to look for him. When they do, he get so mad he spit and spit till de river flood."

"That's how de floods start, Tantie? From Ligahoo's spitting?" Avril asked.

"That's how," Tantie said, and she sighed real soft.

Avril, Cedric, Susan, and I looked at each other and shook our heads. It didn't seem as if anyone could spit enough to make a whole river flood. Tantie must be read our minds 'cause she say, "When fish spit, is a whole lot of water coming from their mouths. Not like if *you* spit."

We figure Tantie know what she talking about, but I'd seen fish before, and I never saw one spit.

Just then, Tantie turned around to say something else, but she just stared and pointed back toward the river. Before we could turn around she shouted, "Oh no, all yuh close your eyes. Close them quick."

"Why, Tantie?" we asked, getting scared because of the look on her face.

"Is Ligahoo! He changing shape. He coming out de river. Close your eyes, I say!"

Avril, Cedric, and Susan closed their eyes fast. Susan shouted, "Tantie, Ligahoo coming? He coming, Tantie?"

"Hush, chile, let me deal with him," Tantie said. "I know him long time. Just don' look."

The last thing I see before I close my eyes was Tantie put her two hands on her hips and square her feet like she mean business.

Then I heard Tantie talking words I couldn't understand. It sounded like magic to me. I just held Susan's and Avril's hands tight and didn't dare open my eyes.

When Tantie finally say that Ligahoo gone back to the river, Avril, Cedric, Susan, and I opened our eyes and ran home fast like a pack of mongoose was on our heels. That was the last time we went down to the river during the rainy season.

Although sometimes we climb up on the roof and look at the river from up there. Tantie say Ligahoo can't see us there but we should still be careful. And if we see a big fish rising up from the river, we must close our eyes and turn in the other direction. That way Ligahoo won't think we looking at him.

The Graveyard Jumbies

ONE DAY, in the middle of our August holidays, Tantie invited me and my cousins to her house.

"We'll have a party," she said. "Bring your pillows."

None of us wanted to go to Tantie's house, especially if it meant we must stay the night.

Tantie live by herself on a lonesome street. At one end is a forgotten graveyard with faded white tombstones sticking out of the ground. Across the street at the other end is Tantie's house. Nothing else is in between except a whole lot of grass and broken street stones.

Tantie used to have neighbors, but they all moved away. People say the graveyard jumbies chased them. Sometimes, if a good sea breeze blowing, we can see leftover pieces of their houses between the tall grasses.

Well, when Mama heard about Tantie's party, she said we had to go. Daddy drove me, Avril, Susan, and Cedric over there, picking up my cousin Gerard on the way. Then Daddy left us standing on Tantie's porch clutching our pillows.

"All yuh come in," said Tantie, throwing wide open the red doors of her wooden house.

We filed inside and put our pillows down on the couch. Tantie doesn't have much furniture. Just that one couch, two wooden rockers, one with a slat missing in the back, and a bamboo table with three chairs. The table was loaded down with food and the smells coming from it made our bellies grumble.

We were standing there taking some good sniffs when Tantie began to laugh. "What wrong with all yuh children?" she asked. "All yuh look like your big toes been stolen and eaten for supper."

I sat down on the edge of the couch and didn't say anything. I didn't want Tantie to know I was scared of the graveyard down the street.

Avril was nervous too, but he's braver than me. He said, "Tantie, it is de jumbies. We 'fraid they go come to de house tonight."

Gerard, Susan, and Cedric nodded their heads. Tantie looked at me, and I nodded mine. I was glad Avril had spoken up, and I could tell the others were too.

Tantie smiled at us and shook her head. "We not worrying 'bout no jumbies tonight," she said. "We just going to eat plenty good food and tell stories."

Then she clapped her hands like that fixed everything and she walked over to the table. She took up a plate from one end and began piling on red beans and rice, curry goat, and big chunks of black puddin'. When her plate was full, she looked at us and said, "All yuh could eat now or later. It don' make me no never mind. But de food will get cold." And with that she sat down in one of the rockers, the one with the missing slat, and ate and rocked, ate and rocked.

Avril, who always goes first, picked up a plate and filled it. Then me and Gerard and Cedric followed. Susan went last, as usual.

Soon we were all busy licking our fingers and going back for more, forgetting about jumbies, graveyards, and everything but the way the food tasted. I was glad we had come to Tantie's party.

When we finished eating, Tantie took our plates into the kitchen and came back carrying a large coconut-currant cake. It was almost three cakes round. None of us had ever seen a cake so big.

"Ohhh, Tantie," I said, eyeing the cake, although my belly was too full for it.

"This is a special cake," said Tantie. "When all yuh eat your slices, be careful."

"Why?" asked Susan, not taking her eyes from the big wonder.

"This cake is full of surprises," said Tantie. "There are presents for everyone inside. If you wish hard when you bite in, you will find yours. De person wishing hardest will find a prize that will start off our storytelling."

When I hear all that talk about presents, my belly suddenly had plenty room again.

"Who wants de first slice?" asked Tantie, holding up a slice of cake as big as a breadfruit.

"Me," we all shouted. Tantie laughed and handed it to Susan.

"We'll go from de littlest to de biggest," she said. Avril groaned because he was the biggest and he wanted his slice right then.

We waited until Tantie had handed out all the slices, then we closed our eyes and wished hard. I wished for a new cricket bat. When I took a big bite, I felt something hard in my mouth. I reached in and pulled out a tiny notebook covered in coconut and currants. I wiped off the cake and opened it. Inside were tiny blank pages. I looked over at Tantie, and she smiled.

"Must mean you go be a writer someday," she said. I smiled back. I liked that idea.

"Look!" shouted Avril, as he pulled a small plastic car from his mouth and wiped off the cake. Avril wants to drive race cars when he gets older.

Gerard found a ring with a bright-red stone in his slice of cake. "That's a ring for a king," I said. Gerard's face broke into a huge smile. He's only seven years old and he thinks he's going to be a king when he gets older, because his last name is Prince.

Then Cedric pulled a beautiful seashell from his slice. "Look," he said, holding it up for us to see. Cedric is a shell collector. He makes gifts from the shells.

But it was Susan who had the best present. When she fished her prize out of her mouth we all gasped. It was a tiny candle wrapped in shiny paper with flowers all over it. The candle was the prettiest thing I had ever seen. It looked like something for a doll's house.

"Well," said Tantie, "who wished de hardest?"

"Me," we answered together. But we all knew it must have been Susan.

Just then the lights in Tantie's house flickered once, twice, and then went off completely. We were standing in pitch-darkness. There were no streetlamps outside to shine in the windows. And there was no moon that night, either.

"Tantie! Tantie! What happen to de lights?" cried Susan.

"I thought this might happen," said Tantie calmly. "They never like to see me have a bit of fun."

"Whatcha talkin' 'bout?" I asked.

"De jumbies, of course," said Tantie. "They pulled de light switches and now current gone. It will take de electric company a long time to fix it."

"Tantie, you said we didn't have to worry 'bout no jumbies to-night," said Cedric.

"I know. But I didn't know we were going to have so much fun.

They only come when I'm having too much fun and they feel left out."

"We not having fun, Tantie," I said, thinking I could trick the jumbies.

"No!" said all my cousins. "Not a bit."

But it wasn't working. The lights were lost to us.

"I know what," said Tantie. "Let's tell a story 'bout those old jumbies. But first, we'll light Susan's candle."

"That candle won't last but two seconds," said Avril.

Tantie didn't say anything. She just lit Susan's tiny candle with a match from her pocket and put it on a small plate. We gathered close together on the mat to hear Tantie's story. The tiny candle sat in the middle of us, glowing small but bright and not flickering a bit. Tantie's eyes were shadowed in the dark and when she looked at me, I felt it more than I could see it.

"Would all yuh like to hear about de jumbies from de grave-yard?" she asked softly.

I shivered and nodded my head. Avril and Cedric and Susan and Gerard must have done the same thing because Tantie started:

"A long, long time ago when I first lived here, this house was only one of de pretty, brightly painted houses on this side of de street. Next to my red house was a big blue house and next to that one was a small pink house and at de end of de street was a large green house. We all grew pretty-colored flowers in our yards because we didn't have any room to grow trees. But that was okay. Across de street there weren't any houses. But de trees. Glory! De trees were tall and wide and greener than any I've seen."

"What happened to them?" asked Avril.

"I'll tell you in a minute, boy. But first, let me tell you there was something else across this street. At de very very end where nobody would bother it was a tiny graveyard with two or three stones. As de years passed, de graveyard did begin to get more and more tombstones. That was still okay. That is, it was okay until people came in and started cutting down all those beautiful trees to make room for new houses. Before long, there was a bright yellow house, then a brown one, and even a purple house across de street. But all de trees were dead and gone just like de folks buried in that grave-yard.

"Well, now I knew trouble coming. Because what most folks don't know is that wherever you have a graveyard, you must have plenty of trees."

"Why, Tantie?" I interrupted.

"Because a graveyard is a jumbies' playground. All those jumbie spirits floating around looking over their bodies buried in de ground sometimes get bored and like to play. So they swing and dance in nearby trees. And they don' bother nobody. In fact, if you want to see a jumbie, all you have to do is climb a tree next to a graveyard and wait for de jumbies to come play.

"Anyway, when folks started cutting down those trees de jumbies lost their favorite place to play. So they crept inside de first house and played there instead. They swung from de lights and danced on de tables. They stole sheets drying on clotheslines and ran around de yard at night waving them and scaring everyone.

"Soon afterwards, de people in that house moved out, and de jumbies, bored because they still had no trees to play in, went on to de second house. They did de same thing there and those folks quickly moved away. And so de jumbies continued their pranks un-til all my neighbors had packed up and moved far away. And no one else ever came to fill the houses. It was too late; de jumbies had already taken over."

"How come you didn't have to move, Tantie?" Susan asked.

"Because I have trees now," she said. "When I saw all de trouble de jumbies were causing, I said to myself, 'It's time to start planting.' And I did. I made room for trees. I planted a mango tree and a lime tree and a tall, skinny coconut tree, which is de jumbies' favorite because they like to shimmy up de trunk and slide down fast fast. Sometimes I can hear them laughing at night as they climb up, up and slide down, down."

"So it worked?" Gerard whispered.

"Well," said Tantie. "Those jumbies peek into my windows every now and then and they pull de electric switches if they think I having fun and they ain't, but otherwise we stay away from each other. They thankful for de trees I planted."

"So, Tantie, those jumbies definitely not coming in here?" I asked.

"Only if those trees fall down," she said.

Then the candle flickered and went out and we were in darkness again. But this time we weren't scared.

Ever since then we like to visit Tantie. And Avril says one night soon we going to climb Tantie's mango tree and wait for the jumbies to come out and play. But I don't know about that!

Simon and the Big Joke

Tᴴɪꜱ ɪꜱʟᴀɴᴅ ɪꜱ ᴛʜᴇ ᴋɪɴᴅ of place where everybody always trying to play a big joke on someone else. Like the time Avril gave me and Susan two plantains and told us they were bananas. We peeled them fast fast and took big bites. Well, plantains look like bananas, but they sure don't taste like them. They're hard and starchy, not sweet at all. Me and Susan spit the plantain out while Avril laughed at us.

But the best big joke I ever heard of was the one Tantie told us about after Avril, Cedric, Susan, and I tried to play one on *her*.

It was the day before my birthday and Tantie had come over to help Mama bake a cake and pies for my party. We knew Tantie would go out into the backyard to pick some mangoes for a pie. We climbed up the mango tree and hid behind the leaves.

When Tantie came outside she carried her long mango-picking pole with her. Then she started hitting the tree with the pole so that mangoes would drop. Each time she hit the tree we yelled, "Ouch!" and "Ahhh!"

Tantie looked up at the tree, wondering where the noises were coming from. We got quiet. When she didn't hear anything, she started back up. "Ouch! Ahhh!" we shouted, each time Tantie hit the tree. Tantie stopped. She looked at the tree trunk and then reached over and patted it.

"Well, Mr. Tree," she said. "I real sorry to bother you and all. I was only trying to pick some of your mangoes to make my good little children sweet mango pies. But it look like they cahn get any now." Then Tantie put her picking pole down and began walking away.

Me, Avril, Cedric, and Susan jumped down from that tree so fast we bring down about ten mangoes with us at the same time.

"Tantie," I called. "It was us in de tree. Come back and pick de mangoes for de pie."

Tantie looked back and she had a big grin on her face. "All yuh cahn get your Tantie in a big joke. It was I who fool all yuh. I knew you up there. All yuh think Tantie don' know nothing?"

Then as Tantie took her picking pole up from the ground, she said, "I must tell all yuh 'bout de time an old man try to fool your Tantie. I get him back good. Nobody cahn play a big joke on *me*. I live too long for that to happen."

Well, when we hear that we sat down on the ground. We watched as Tantie banged the pole on the tree and listened as she told her story. It turned out to be one of Tantie's best stories ever, because it had my own mama in it.

"One day," Tantie began, "when Amber's mama was 'bout ten years old, I took her for a boat ride to Tobago. It was a big boat with plenty people up on deck watching de waves hit de boat belly with loud booms. Near us was an old man with a monkey on his shoulder. It look like de man was quarreling with de monkey cause we hear him shouting. Then all of a sudden he said in a louder voice, 'Does anybody want this monkey? They can have him for one dollar.'

"Well, who tell him say that! Sylvie ran over quick quick and pulled out de dollar I had given her for sno-cones. De man looked at her and said, 'Now, this monkey is pretty special. His name is Simon and he talks.'

"Everybody on deck came hurrying over to see if they could get de monkey now. Nobody think to ask *how* this monkey could talk.

"Sylvie handed de man her dollar and took de monkey. De man said again, 'Simon can talk like a real person.'"

"Monkeys cahn talk, Tantie," I interrupted.

"Monkeys cahn talk, eh?" said Tantie, and she picked up a big mango from the pile on the ground and examined it.

"Anyway, it was Sylvie who got a good hold of de monkey and wouldn't let go.

"'Simon, honey,' she coo coo at him, holding him in her arms like he a baby.

"'What?' said a croaky old voice.

"Sylvie was so surprised she almost dropped de monkey. My mouth fell wide open. I know de man said that de monkey could speak, but didn't none of us expect to hear him so plain plain.

"Then we heard it again. 'What? You call my name and don' say nothin'.'

"'Well, look at that,' said a woman. 'That monkey rude for so. He giving backchat.'

"It was true. De monkey could talk, but he was very rude. 'Sylvie, do-do darlin',' I said, 'why you don' give de monkey to me?'

"'No, Tantie,' she said, holding Simon so tight that he yelled, 'What you squeezing me so for? You think I'm a breadfruit?'

"Everybody on the boat deck started to laugh.

"'Tantie, Simon is mine and I keeping him,' Sylvie shouted over the laughter.

"I looked around for Simon's owner. He was standing by de railing with a big smile on his face like he really enjoying himself.

"'Okay, Sylvie,' I said. 'You can keep de monkey, but we go have to teach him some manners.'

"Sylvie didn't hear me. She was coo cooing at her monkey again.

"'Oh, Simon,' she said, stroking his ears.

"'Whatcha keep on calling my name for?' said de monkey.

"'I just trying it out,' said poor Sylvie.

"'Well, try it out later. I want to sleep now.'

"Sylvie nodded her head and cuddled Simon closer.

"'And stop choking me like that,' said Simon. 'I need to breathe.'

"I couldn't listen to the two of them any longer. 'Simon,' I said to myself, 'you'se a real humbug.'"

Tantie stopped talking to tie up the hem of her apron. Then she put two mangoes into the apron-basket she had made.

"So what happen next, Tantie?" I asked.

"I let Sylvie keep him of course," said Tantie. "She looked so pleased with her pet that I didn't have de heart to say no."

"But Tantie," I said, "you didn't say how de monkey learn to talk."

"I getting to that, chile. Hold your horses."

Tantie picked up some more mangoes and put them in her apron.

"I figured that as soon as I could get Simon's owner alone, I would ask him how to fix de monkey's rudeness. He would know, I thought. But every time I tried to speak to him, he ducked out of sight. And when I turned back around, there he was standing near Sylvie and Simon. Poor man was finding it hard to part with his monkey.

"Finally, I was able to grab him by his shirttails and hold on for dear life. 'Mister,' I said, 'please show me how to teach that monkey some manners. He have de rudest mouth I ever hear.'

"De man tugged his shirttails out of my hand. Then he put his hands on his hips and glared at me. 'That monkey no more ruder than you,' he said. 'Leave me alone.'

"'But sir, my niece is only ten years old.'

"'So,' he snorted, and marched off.

"Well, I could see where Simon learned his manners. Then something dawned in my mind. No, I thought. That can't be. But I decided to keep an eye on that old man.

"I watched him walk over to where Sylvie was standing. She was in de middle of a group of people. They were stroking de monkey's head and tail. They were trying to get him to speak, but it looked like Simon didn't have anything to say. Then when Simon's owner had edged up to the group, de monkey suddenly started talking again.

"'Stop touching me,' he said. 'Whatcha think I is—a doll?'

"And that's when I figured out how Simon could talk."

"How?" Avril asked, looking up at Tantie. But Tantie smiled and continued her story.

"I decided to try an experiment. I walked over to Sylvie and said, 'Honey, let us go downstairs and have lunch. We can ask Simon what he wants to eat.'

"Before anyone could say anything, I took Sylvie's arm and we were gone. We went downstairs to a corner of the huge dining room, and sat at a table. Nobody could come near us without us seeing them first. We sat there for a long time and asked Simon plenty questions. But he didn't say one word. And he wasn't sleeping either. De monkey was jumping all over de chairs and table and twirling his little hands in our hair.

"Sylvie started to fret because she thought he was sick. 'Why he not talking?' she wondered.

"'Honey, he don' look sick to me,' I said.

"Then I saw Simon's owner coming near. He was inching up to our table as if he had something to hide from. But I said loudly, 'Hello, Mister.' And he jumped.

"'Hi,' he said.

"When he got close to de table, Simon suddenly said, 'All yuh call this lunch? I ain't even had my bananas yet.'

"Sylvie squealed happily. But when I heard Simon, I knew my idea was right."

"What idea, Tantie?" I asked.

"About how Simon could talk, of course," said Tantie.

"I put my hand in Sylvie's hand and squeezed it, telling her silently not to say anything. She understood because she let me do de talking.

"'Mister,' I said, 'your monkey just couldn't stop talking all through lunch. He 'bout talk our ears off.'

"De man got a funny look on his face. 'Simon was talking?' he whispered.

"'Yes,' I answered. Sylvie nodded her head in agreement. 'All through lunch he just wouldn't stop.'

"'But—but he couldn't,' said de man.

"'What do you mean?' I asked.

"'He couldn't have spoken to you.'

"People from de top deck had slowly gathered around our table and was listening to de conversation.

"'Why couldn't he have spoken?' said one man. 'I heard him speak earlier.'

"'Yes,' said another. 'We heard him with our own ears.'

"'Well, yes,' said Simon's owner. 'But he can't speak if I'm not here.'

"'Well, he was telling me all kinds of things just now,' piped up Sylvie.

"'I heard him myself,' said a woman at de next table, who winked at me when she said it.

"But de old man hadn't seen her wink, and what she said so frightened him that he snatched up Simon and ran out of de room.

"I burst out laughing and couldn't stop for a long time. Sylvie and de people were asking me what was going on, and I could barely stop laughing to tell them.

"My idea *was* right. Simon's owner was de one making Simon talk. He was throwing his voice so it sounded like it was coming from de monkey. We thought it was Simon speaking, but it was really only de owner. And he was being mighty rude to little Sylvie.

"'He won't be playing that trick for a while,' said a woman, chuckling.

"'No,' I said, putting my arm around Sylvie. 'But poor Sylvie had to pay a whole dollar for that trickster to learn a lesson.'"

Tantie stopped picking up the mangoes and looked at us.

"So Tantie, you's de smartest one on that boat?" Avril asked.

"Not de smartest, chile. But I do keep my wits on me, and ain't no trickster going to fool Tantie. All yuh remember that, too."

Tantie headed back to the house with her apron full of mangoes. As she walked she said over her shoulder, "Anybody wanting some sweet mango pies tomorrow better come in and help Tantie peel these mangoes. Birthday girl too."

We got up off the ground and ran after Tantie. None of us wanted to miss out on Tantie's pies. But I bet all of us were thinking the same thing: What big joke could we play on Tantie to fool her good! Something is bound to come up, although Mama says she and *her* cousins been trying to fool Tantie for a long, long time and haven't done it yet.

A Wave in Her Pocket

ONE EASTER HOLIDAY, Daddy decided to take the whole family on a trip to Toco. Toco is a beach on the northeastern tip of the island. My cousins and I had never gone there because it's not the best place for a sea bath.

"Too many rocks," said Uncle Rupert.

"And clumpy sand," said Auntie Hazel.

"And waves too big to jump over," added Mama.

Still, Daddy wanted us to go because Toco is one of the prettiest places to see.

We left early in the morning. The sun had just started lighting up the tops of the coconut trees. They looked like giant candles. Daddy packed up our car with Mama in the front seat, and me, Susan, and Cedric in the back.

Aunts and uncles and other cousins packed up their cars too. When everyone was ready, we drove off down the narrow pitch road, one behind the other like a trail of goats.

At first, Cedric, Susan, and I had plenty room in the backseat. But then Daddy pulled up in front of Tantie's home. The five other cars parked behind Daddy, filling up Tantie's empty street. Tantie sat waiting on her bright red porch.

"Where Tantie go sit?" asked Susan.

Nobody answered. We knew Tantie would pick the car *she* wanted to ride in. We watched as she climbed down her front steps slow slow. She was carrying a basket bigger than two of me. And she was heading for our car.

"Well, is now de backseat go get crowded," said Cedric.

"Shush," Mama said, as Daddy got out and helped Tantie in. She squeezed in between me and Cedric and placed her basket smack-dab on her lap. We could barely see each other over the big basket. I hoped Tantie would open it up and share out some black cake or plums. But Tantie sat there like she was at the movies, her two eyes staring straight ahead, as Daddy drove down the street.

"What wrong with Tantie?" Cedric whispered behind her head.

I shrugged.

Susan said, "Tantie, why you don't tell us a story?"

But for the first time ever, Tantie shook her head. "No stories today, dear."

Mama and Daddy were singing aloud to old calypso playing on the radio so I guess they didn't notice that Tantie was acting strange and looking sad. I decided to cheer her up, and Susan and Cedric must have had the same idea.

Susan said, "Look, Tantie," and pointed to a boy walking at the side of the road with five baby goats following him. But Tantie didn't even look.

Then Cedric said, "Tantie, I think I go win de marble-pitching contest at school." But Tantie didn't even say, "Good luck."

Then I said, "Tantie, you lived in Toco when you were little. It have plenty fun things to do there?" Tantie acted like she didn't hear a word I said.

Suddenly, Daddy rounded a bend in the road. We started driving down into a beautiful valley. The sea sprang up all around. It was sparkling like a blue Carnival costume. The waves were smacking the rocks with big kisses and then ducking back into the sea. The trees were green and spread out wide like fans. Even the rocks looked different here. They jutted out from the land like big, brown fishermen waiting to catch fish.

It seemed like all this prettiness woke Tantie up. She stopped sitting still and started looking around. She looked out Susan's window and smiled at the trees and the sky. She looked out the front window and smiled at the next hill coming up. Then she looked out my window where the blue sea was shining in the sunlight, and her smiled disappeared clean off her face.

"Tantie, what's wrong?" I asked.

Tantie just stared and stared at the sea. Then the strangest thing happened. A tear rolled down her face. It was just me who saw. I didn't know what to do. I put my head on Tantie's shoulder and squeezed her hand real tight.

Daddy drove up and down one hill after another. Each valley was prettier than the one before. I didn't look at Tantie anymore but I could feel her staring out my window.

Finally, we reached Toco. The first thing I saw as Daddy parked the car was a huge turtle walking on the sand. His head was out of his shell and he was looking all around. When he saw us, though, he stuck his head quick quick back in his shell and sat on the beach like a rock. Tantie saw this and laughed. I laughed too, 'cause I was happy to see Tantie not sad anymore. Cedric and Susan and Mama and Daddy started laughing also. When everybody else arrived they thought we were a bunch of crazies because we were sitting on the beach laughing at a rock.

After a while Mama and Daddy and Auntie Hazel and the rest of the family gathered the picnic baskets and climbed over the rocks to find a good place to eat. I decided to stay by the turtle to see if he'd stick his head back out. Tantie stayed too.

She sat down next to the turtle. "Hello!" she shouted, and bent her face close. I was sitting on the other side of the turtle. He was so big it looked like Tantie and I were at a table for two.

"Tell him hello," said Tantie.

"Hello, Mr. Turtle," I shouted and patted him on his hard old shell.

Then Tantie said, "He remind me of a story. Want to hear?"

I was so glad that Tantie had changed her mind about not telling any stories today that I couldn't answer. I just nodded my head and Tantie began her tale.

"A long time ago, a young girl lived by a deep blue sea like this one. She had brown skin like de rocks, long braids like de seaweed, and everyone said her eyes were like de midnight wave.

"This girl loved de sea and de sea animals more than anything else. She loved de seashells, and de starfish, de snails, and de sand dollars. She even loved de yellow sand crabs that no one else liked. Her favorite, however, was de big old turtles. She called them her grandfathers.

"These turtles came out only at night. During de day they hid themselves by de rocks so no one could see them. But de girl figured out a way. She climbed on top a tall, smooth rock that overhung de rocks where de turtles hid and she dropped small fish below. Then she waited on her rock and watched as turtle heads popped out to snap up de fish. Each day de girl took them fish to eat and after a while de grandfather turtles began waiting for her.

"As de girl grew older she began to love something even more than her grandfather turtles. Actually, it was someone. His name was Godfrey and he was a young fisherman. Every morning de girl stood on de beach and watched Godfrey set out in his little pirogue. And every afternoon she waited for him to pull in his nets.

"In her mind she said, 'Hello, Godfrey.' And in her mind he answered, 'Hello Delphine.' But she never said it out loud."

"Tantie," I interrupted excitedly. "Isn't Delphine your name too?"

"Yes, chile, it is," said Tantie. Then she went on.

"After Godfrey put his fish into big baskets and sold them to de village women, he tied up his pirogue and walked home. When he passed Delphine he smiled, and his face glowed like de sun.

"Delphine knew there was no one else like him. And she also knew that just like de waves would always come one after de other, she and Godfrey would be together forever."

"Tantie," I interrupted again. "This not de kind of story you usually tell."

Tantie nodded her head. "I guess 'cause this not really a made-up one, chile."

"Whatcha mean, Tantie? It for true?"

Tantie only smiled and put her finger to her lips to shush me. Then she went on.

"One morning around this same time of year when de villagers were planning a big Easter celebration, Delphine watched Godfrey set out in his pirogue. But this time she felt a darkness deep down inside herself. She stepped up to him and, for the first time ever, touched his hand.

"'Don't go,' she said in her mind. She looked in his eyes and saw de sea. And his smile was better than de sun. But she couldn't say her words out loud. She stepped back and let him go."

"How come she couldn't talk?" I asked, forgetting all about Tantie's shush finger. "Was she scared that Godfrey wouldn't listen to her?"

Tantie smiled slowly. "Yes, I think that's why. Anyway, let me tell de rest of de story.

"That afternoon Delphine waited and waited for Godfrey to come back. She climbed on top her high rock and shaded her eyes from de sun. She looked and looked, but she couldn't see anything but waves.

"De next afternoon Delphine climbed on top her rock again. She waited and waited. She even forgot to feed de turtles. But Godfrey still didn't come. Every day she climbed de rock and looked at de sea for Godfrey. But only de waves looked back at her. Then one day as she stood on her rock, Delphine thought she heard de waves singing a song.

"I'll marry my love, the deep blue sea,
And carry him in my pocket.
I'll marry my love
And carry my love,
A wonderful wave in my pocket."

"Tantie, what that song mean? How can you carry a wave in your pocket?" I asked.

"That's what Delphine wondered, too," said Tantie. "She thought it was a song from Godfrey but she didn't know what it meant."

"Well, did she ever figure it out?" I asked, looking at the big waves splashing onto the sand.

"No," said Tantie sadly. "She never figured it out. After a while she stopped climbing de rock. And she moved far away to a town with plenty people, and streets instead of sand, and cars instead of pirogues. But especially no waves to sing that song to her."

Tantie looked out over the sea.

"Tantie," I said softly. "Are you de same Delphine in de story?"

Even though I had guessed it, I was surprised when she nodded her head. Poor Tantie. I listened to the waves hitting the sand until it sounded as if they were singing Tantie's song.

"Tantie, I think I know what that song means," I said slowly.

Tantie looked up at me with a funny expression on her face. Like she had forgotten I was there. "Okay, Amber, tell me what it means," she answered. I could see her eyes were still far away.

"Well," I said. "De song says 'I'll marry my love, the deep blue sea, and carry him in my pocket.' And you said that you loved de sea *and* you loved Godfrey. Well, when Godfrey never came back from de sea, he was part of de sea. So, 'my love, the deep blue sea' means him, Godfrey." I patted the turtle on his hard shell and hoped Tantie was understanding me.

"Marrying someone means that person will always be right next to you, and carrying something in your pocket means de same thing. So, when de song said to marry your love and carry him in your pocket, it meant to keep Godfrey close to you always. Like in your heart, I guess." I glanced over at Tantie. "And it's a happy song, not a sad one, because it called Godfrey a wonderful wave in your pocket. So de sea was singing a song from Godfrey to you saying to never forget him and to keep him close always."

Well, when I finish that long speech, Tantie's face was shining bright bright.

"Amber," she said. "You alone done figure it out." And she got up and gave me a big hug. I was so happy that I forgot sometimes I'm a little bit afraid of her and I hugged her back hard. Then she grabbed my hand. "Come on," she said. "Let's you and me go dip our arms in de water and give Godfrey de sea a hug. Then we go find your mama and them so we can eat!"

And that's just what me and Tantie did.

The Bamboo Beads

LAST YEAR DURING the planting season, I helped Mama plant seeds on our hill. "One seed for each of my brothers and sisters," she said, and she covered up seven seeds with dark dirt. Mama's family lives on the other side of the island, so we hardly ever see them.

Each day I watched Mama water the dark mounds of dirt and weed around them. Soon, flowers grew up. They were red as the evening sun. But one day the floods came and swept them to the sea.

"Poor Mama," I said.

"They'll grow again," she replied.

She looked at her gardening gloves hanging on a nail. "If they don't grow back, we'll plant some more." And she smiled.

That night the moon was round and white as my Sunday hat. I told Daddy how Mama's flowers had drowned in the flood rains. He said, "Did I ever show you how *I* count my brothers and sisters?"

"No," I answered.

Then Daddy showed me the fisherman stars. "They point fishermen to the way home," he said. "There are eight of them. I named one each for my brothers and sisters."

"How do you know which is which?" I asked.

Daddy pointed again to the bright stars. "Well, there's Rupert and Hazel, Anthony and Derek, Peter, Janet, and Neil."

"You forgot Auntie Sonia," I said.

Daddy smiled and pointed to a tiny star. "That one's her."

I nodded my head as Daddy moved his finger around although I couldn't tell which star was who.

After that, Daddy and I looked for the fisherman stars each night. Some nights when the sea breezes blew dark clouds in the sky, we couldn't see them. But Daddy would say, "They'll come back." And he'd smile.

"I wish I had brothers and sisters to plant flowers for or to count stars on," I told Mama and Daddy one day. "I'm tired of having only myself."

"What about all your cousins?" asked Mama.

"You can count them on something," said Daddy.

"What can I count them on?" I wondered.

"Maybe Tantie can help find you something," said Mama. "She's the one who keeps track of all yuh."

So, the next time Tantie came to visit, I said, "Tantie, Mama said you keep track of me and my cousins."

"That's right, chile," said Tantie. "And is plenty of all yuh to keep track of, too."

"I know," I said, "but how you do it? I want something that I can name after each one of my cousins. Something I can count them on. Like Mama has flowers and Daddy has his fisherman stars."

Well, Tantie looked me in the eye for a long time. Then from underneath the neck of her dress she pulled out a brown string full of bright, colorful beads.

"Tantie, where you get those pretty beads from?" I asked.

"These, my dear, is a story by itself, and if you have de time to listen, I'll tell it to you."

I nodded and sat down on the porch swing next to Tantie. As Tantie told her story, I kept trying to push the swing with my foot. But Tantie was too heavy. The swing sat quiet quiet. The only sound was Tantie's voice.

"A long, long time ago," she began, "when I was in my bare feet still, I went to market with a basket of bread and red-currant buns to sell. Market day was de busiest time. There was plenty to see as I set up my little stall and tucked cloths around de bread and buns so de flies wouldn't get them.

"I hadn't sold one thing yet when an old man came up. His clothes were ragged and he didn't have on no shoes. His feet didn't look like no ordinary feet. They looked like cow hooves. I didn't stare, though, because it rude to do that.

"He asked for a piece of bread. Well, I remember Mama telling me that morning to get good prices for de bread, but I was sure Mama hadn't meant from this man too. So, I cut off a hunk of bread, wrapped it in brown paper, and handed it to him. He looked so hungry that I reached for a bun and gave him that too. De man smiled and bowed his head at me. Then he went his way.

"After that I was busy selling bread. De buns went even faster. By afternoon, I had sold them all. Then I saw de old man coming over again. He didn't look so ragged anymore. His hair was combed and he had on a new shirt.

"'I'm sorry,' I said. 'No more bread left.'

"He didn't answer. Instead he handed me something. It was a piece of brown string. It looked like an ordinary old string, but I didn't tell him that.

"'Thank you for de bread, child,' he said. Then he shuffled off and was gone.

"I looked at de string for a while. I could use it to tie up my bread cloths, I thought. Or I could use it as a hair ribbon. But I decided I would put de string around my neck and wear it like a necklace."

"This de same string, Tantie?" I asked, fingering Tantie's bead necklace.

"De very same," she answered.

"Well, that evening, Mama was so proud I had sold all de bread that she gave me a treat. It was a small blue bamboo bead. It was de exact color of Mama's best blue head scarf.

"'Where you get this bead, Mama?' I asked.

"'Found it in de yard,' she replied.

"I wondered how it got there but it didn't matter. I pulled out my brown string and untied it. Then I slipped de blue bead on and tied it around my neck again. It looked like a real necklace now that it had Mama's bead on it."

"Is this your mama's bead?" I asked, touching a bright blue bead on Tantie's string.

"Yes, that's it, chile," said Tantie. "And it shines more now than de day I got it.

"Two days later, Daddy found a smooth black bead down by de sea. He brought it home in his pocket.

"'I thought you might like this,' he said and handed it to me. It sparkled like a black sun. I untied my necklace and slipped it on next to de blue bead. Now my string was beautiful with Mama's and Daddy's bamboo beads on it.

"During de next few days, Mama and Daddy and I kept finding shiny bamboo beads in de strangest places. I found a red one under de bed. Mama found a green one in de garden, and Daddy found a yellow one in his shoe. Mama and Daddy didn't think nothing of it but as I added each new bead to my necklace, I got a strange, trembly feeling.

"De next week when I took Mama's bread and currant buns to market, I saw de old man who had given me my string. His clothes were still ragged and he clumped around on his hooves.

"'Hello, mister,' I said when he came over. I wrapped up a chunk of bread and two buns this time and gave them to him. He smiled and shuffled off.

"Again my day of selling flew by. Before lunchtime I had sold everything. Mama hugged me hard when I got home. But then she sat down at de kitchen table and looked serious.

"'What's wrong?' I asked.

"'Look,' she said, pointing to a bowl on the table. I looked inside and there were de most beautiful, shiny bamboo beads I'd ever seen. Lots and lots of them. I put my hand in and touched de smooth wood.

"'Where they come from?' I asked.

"'Don't know,' said Mama. 'They were here when I turned around from de sink this morning. I thought you might know something about them, since you're collecting beads.'

"'No,' I said. 'I don't know about these.'

"Then Mama said, 'Let me see that string of beads around your neck, girl.'

"I showed it to Mama. She looked and looked at de beads and tugged on de string until I thought she'd break it. Then she looked at me and said, 'You've met Papa Bois.'

"'Papa who?'

"'Papa Bois,' she murmured. 'He lives in de forest and protects de trees and forest animals from hunters. He spends his time whittling bamboo beads from fallen bamboo shoots. He's de only one who could make these beads. They're priceless.'

"Mama looked at me and gave me back de necklace. 'Have you met an old man without any feet?' she asked.

"I immediately thought of de old man from de market. 'Yes, Mama, I met him last week at de market. An old man in ragged clothes and no feet. He had cow hooves instead.'

"Mama closed her eyes and nodded her head. 'That's Papa Bois,' she said. 'He can be dangerous. Once he meets someone, he keeps track of them by counting their sins, their blessings, even their teeth, on his whittled beads. You never know with Papa Bois just what he's counting for you. The last time Papa Bois gave someone beads, the beads represented de number of days he had left to live. These beads on de table must be for you. He's counting something for you.'"

"'What?' I whispered, almost too frightened to speak.

"'We won't know till he's ready to say. Were you kind or mean to him?'

"'I gave him some bread to eat because he looked hungry,' I said.

"'Good,' said Mama, and she pulled me into her arms. 'That was very kind. Now you might as well put de beads on de string and wait until Papa Bois comes back and tells you what he's counting.'

"I put de pretty beads on de string. I didn't think they would all fit, but no matter how many I put on, de string never filled up. When every bead was on I counted thirty-three beads. Then I tied it around my neck once more. It wasn't any heavier than when I wore de string empty.

"As de days passed, Mama, Daddy, and I kept our eyes open for Papa Bois. We thought he might come by anytime. I wondered over and over what Papa Bois could be counting on my beads."

"Were you scared, Tantie?" I interrupted.

"A little," she answered. "But I knew I had been kind to Papa Bois, and that was all that mattered.

"De next time I went to market for Mama, she wanted to come with me. I told her Papa Bois might not come to our stall if she was there.

At the stall I laid de bread and buns out nicely and covered them with clothes. I saw de old man shuffling up to my table.

" '*Bonjour, vieux Papa,*' I said. Mama had told me that to say hello in French was de polite way to greet Papa Bois. She also said not to look at his feet no matter what.

" '*Bonjour,*' said de old man.

" 'Would you like some bread?' I asked. Papa Bois nodded.

"As I cut him a chunk of bread, I said, 'Thank you for de pretty necklace.'

" 'It's for you to wear always,' he said. 'Until you find someone who should wear it instead.'

"Papa Bois' eyes looked kind in his wrinkled face. I decided I go ask him what de beads were for.

" 'De beads,' he answered, 'are for all de little children you'll one day have.'

" 'Thirty-three children?' I asked.

" 'Yes, they'll be yours, but they won't be yours,' " he said mysteriously. But then he smiled a big smile.

" 'All right,' " I said, and I handed him de bread and buns.

"That was de last time I ever see Papa Bois. Mama said he only comes out of his forest when he's lonely for human company. Otherwise his friends are de deer, de squirrels, and de trees. The first person he meets when he leaves his forest early in de morning is de one who counts. If that person stares at his feet or laughs at him— watch out!"

"But Tantie, what happen to de thirty-three children?" I asked.

"You're one of them," she said. "Ever since your oldest cousin Jarise was born, I been de one helping to take care of all yuh. I have thirty grandnieces and nephews now. That mean three more to come. And all yuh are *my* children, just like Papa Bois said."

Tantie reached up and unhooked her bamboo bead necklace. Then she laid it in my hands.

"Oh," I said, looking at Tantie's necklace again. "I'd like to be de red bead."

Tantie took the necklace out of my hands and put it around my neck. She tied the string. The necklace felt cool and smooth against my skin.

"I wish I had a mirror," I said.

"It looking beautiful," said Tantie. "And it for you now. You can count your cousins on them beads."

"You're giving this to me, Tantie?" I asked, not believing what I had heard.

"Papa Bois said I go find someone who should wear it."

"Thank you," I said. I ran my fingers over the bamboo smoothness of the beads and admired the pretty colors.

"And since you wear Papa Bois' beads, you can start helping me tell these stories," said Tantie. "I been doing de work alone for too long."

Tantie reached over and adjusted the bead string on my neck.

I looked down at the shiny red bead that was me and smiled and smiled.

Afterword

No collection of stories about Trinidad would be complete without some of the well-known figures from the island's rich folklore, like the Soucouyant, Ligahoo, and Papa Bois. Most of these legendary characters are of African origin and were brought to the island by slaves long ago. Trinidad's folklore is also heavily influenced by the many other cultures that comprise the island's population—Indian, Chinese, Spanish, French, and English.

These folklore characters play an important role in the lives of Trinidadians. They may be blamed for unexplained deaths, missing people, even a severe flood. And often they appear in stories told to teach children a lesson, like the danger of staying out late or playing near rivers during the rainy season. But for many Trinidadians, these characters are not merely figures in a story. They are real. And many a Trinidadian can point out the soucouyant or ligahoo of his or her village.

The name *soucouyant,* pronounced "soo KEE ya," is derived from the French word *soupçonnant,* "suspecting"—specifically, suspecting a person of being a witch. The soucouyant is usually an old woman of the village who lives alone and is seldom seen in the daytime. She is believed to sleep during the day and change into a ball of flame at night. She flies through the sky looking for an unsuspecting human whose blood she will suck, as does the vampire in European folklore.

To discover who the soucouyant of a village is, you must empty one hundred pounds of rice at the village crossroads. The soucouyant will be compelled to stop and pick up the rice one grain at a time. To kill a soucouyant, you can drown her in the tide, or if you can find where she has put her skin at night, you may cover it with salt so that it will burn her when she tries to put it on in the morning.

Like the soucouyant, the ligahoo has great supernatural powers. The spelling and pronunciation of this creature's name are derived from the French words *loup garou,* meaning werewolf, and in Trinidad the name is pronounced "LAG a hoo." Ligahoo is the name given to the old medicine man of a village. Like medicine men in many other cultures, Ligahoo is well respected and feared. He can proclaim curses as well as offer protection. Ligahoo's greatest power is his ability to change his shape. This shape-changing power is believed to be hereditary in some old Creole families. To see a ligahoo without him seeing you, you must take some yampee ("sleep") from the corner of a dog's eye and put it in your own eye. Then at midnight, peep out of a keyhole.

The most popular of all of Trinidad's folklore characters is Papa Bois (the name is pronounced "Papa Boy"). Papa Bois is the protector of the trees and animals in the woods. He is known to carry a cow's horn and will blow it to warn animals of approaching hunters. He will often appear to a hunter in the shape of a deer and lead him deep into the woods, where he'll resume his true shape and give a strict warning.

Papa Bois's true shape is that of an old man dressed in ragged clothes. His beard has leaves growing out of it, and his feet are cloven hoofs. If you meet Papa Bois, you must greet him politely in French: *"Bonjour, vieux Papa"* ("Good day, venerable Papa") or *"Bon matin, Maître"* ("Good morning, Master"). And if he talks to you, you should remain calm, and *never* look at his feet.

Glossary

Bacchanal—Confusion, chaos.

Black puddin'—A sausage filled with pig's blood; a delicacy in the islands.

Calypso—A form of folk music that originated in Trinidad using African rhythms. Calpyso songs are made up on the spot by the singer; they are funny and usually about current events.

Carnival—A two-day festival, held before the beginning of Lent, in which steel bands and dancers wearing elaborate colorful costumes parade through the streets.

Cricket wickets—Wooden poles used as the "bases" in the game of cricket.

Chip-chip—Shellfish similar to mussels, used in broths.

Coal pots—Big, blackened pots that sit over coals.

Do-do—An endearment, like "darling" or "dear"; pronounced "doo-doo."

Jumbies—Bogeymen or ghosts.

Plantain—A vegetable that looks like a banana but is hard and starchy. It's usually cooked before it is eaten.

Pirogue—A small boat used by fishermen.

LYNN JOSEPH was born and raised on the island of Trinidad in the West Indies. She grew up listening to stories like the ones in this book. Ms. Joseph moved to the United States with her family and was graduated from the University of Colorado. She now lives in New York City, where she is raising her son, Jared, and studying at Fordham University School of Law. She is the author of *Coconut Kind of Day: Island Poems* (Lothrop). *A Wave in Her Pocket* is her first book for Clarion.

BRIAN PINKNEY was born in Boston, Massachusetts, and was graduated from Philadelphia College of Art with a Bachelor of Fine Arts degree. He developed the distinctive scratchboard technique used in this book while studying at the School of Visual Arts, where he received a Master of Fine Arts degree in illustration. Mr. Pinkney's illustrations have appeared in newspapers and national magazines and in three previous children's books. Mr. Pinkney lives in New York City.